BUDDY ONIONRING'S

HORRIBLE
Halloween
Jokes for Kids

First Edition

Buddy Onionring

ISBN: 9781695487949

Table of Contents

Buddy Onionring

Small Jokes

Why did the gremlin get fired from the cookie factory?

He kept goblin them up.

What kind of spa will grant you five wishes?

A monkey spa

Who is a jack-o'-lantern's favorite comedian?

Dana Carvey

Have you heard about the fake jack-o'-lanterns?

They can't hold a candle to the real ones.

How did the ghoul get vegetables?
He gruesome.

Buddy Onionring

BIG Jokes

Where can you find out more about giant spiders?
On the World Wide Web

Did you hear the gossip about The Blob?
It's all over town!

What's as big as King Kong but doesn't weigh anything?
King Kong's shadow

Which monster can do the most sit-ups?
The Abdominal Snowman

Buddy Onionring

Medium Jokes

How does the Medium stay in shape?

Plenty of exorcise

What are the chances of getting through a seance without being covered in ectoplasm?

Slime to none

What do you call the spirit of an angry chicken?

A Poultry-geist

How does the psychic know when her kids will cry?

She has a crystal bawl.

When does a ghost receive Workers Compensation?

When they've been conjured on the job.

When does a ghost ask for breakfast?
Every moaning

What job are people dying to get?
Ghost writer

What did the ghost say to her favorite
author?
I'm your biggest phantom!

What do the ghost cheerleaders say?
We got spirit, yes we do! We got spirit,
How about BOO!

How are ghosts able fly?

By booking their seats well in advance

Buddy Onionring

MONSTERS
of
Monster Jokes

What's the Swamp Creature's favorite soup?

Spicy Black Legume

What does Renfield order at a Mexican restaurant?

The Tarantu-lada

What's a werewolf's favorite cartoon?

Transformers

What did the vampire say when he walked into the wrong crypt?

It's not my vault!

What did the bride of Dracula say when he was too tired to bite her?

Fangs for nothing!

In his spare time,
what does the Mummy collect?

Dust.

Why did Dracula leave the poker game?

They kept raising the stakes.

Who picks the Creature from the Black
Lagoon up from school?
His crawdad

What is the Wolfman's favorite
Whitney Houston song?
Howl I know?

How did the Invisible Man's wife know
he was lying?
She could see right through him.

What did the Son of Dracula learn
in kindergarden?
The Alpha-bit

What is Frankenstein's favorite
type of music?
Ska

What happened when the Bride broke up
with Frankenstein's Monster?

He went to pieces.

So his heart was broken?

Yes, but Dr. Frankenstein had three spares.

Does The Monster have anyone
else to date?

Yes, some of the villagers still
carry a torch for him.

What does Dracula love about Transylvania?

The land's cape

When does a werewolf eat cereal?

Whenever he sees a full spoon.

Did you hear they are remaking The Creature From the Black Lagoon in the Atlantic Ocean?

WATER THEY THINKING??

Have you heard how over-worked the Creature is?

He's really been swamped.

Buddy Onionring

Witch Jokes?

Why did the Horror Hostess return her new dress?

It had a terror.

What does the Horror Hostess serve with fried chicken?

Corn on macabre

Why does the witch buy two of every outfit?

She has a twin sinister.

Why can't she buy her own clothes?

She's down on her yuck.

Why don't the two witches live together?

There's just not enough broom.

What offense got the little witch thrown out of Sunday school?

Cursing

What is the Banshee's favorite dessert?

I scream

Buddy Onionring

Graveyard Goofs

When does the mortician do her best work?

In the mourning

How does the mortician know when someone is walking down the hall?

Creepy floorboards

How many setting are on the mortician's thermostat?

Just two: Worm or Ghoul.

When does the gravedigger know it's time to clean up the graveyard?

Whenever it gets tomb messy

Did you hear about the zombie who lost
her glasses and walked right into
an open grave?
She was blurried alive.

Why did the mortician's girlfriend leave him?
He had some skeletons in the closet.

Who is the mortician's favorite comedian?
Dana Ghouled

Why does the morticians car win every race?
It has plenty of hearse-power.

What does the mortician always bring
to the potluck?

Gravy

Why was the shrouded mummy
angry at his insurance company?

They said he wasn't covered.

What does the mortician's daughter get
when she misbehaves?

Five minutes in the Coroner.

Why did the mama ghoul change the
baby ghoul's diaper?

He creeped his pants.

Buddy Onionring

Tales of Spookery

Where does every monster go
to see and be seen?
The Eye Ball

Have you been to it?
No, let's go take a look!

Why did the scarecrow quit his job?

He was in the wrong field.

What does Van Helsing, the vampire
hunter do for fun?

He goes roller-staking.

Why is the werewolf store so small?

It's a gnaw and paw shop.

Did you hear the Jack-o'-lantern's
cousin started lifting weights?

Now he has a pumped kin.

What is Norman Bates' favorite thing about doing laundry?

The spin psycho

What did the executioner give his twin daughters for Christmas?

A pair of shocks

Why does the dungeon master hate his job?

It's the pits.

How does the dungeon master get his torture devices so cheaply?

They're maiden China.

Where did the rabid dog get her new sweater?

At the maul

When can a cow change into a wolf?

On a full MOOOOOON!

Where do zombies kiss at the
Christmas party?

Under the missing toe

What side of the zombie has the
grossest sores?

The Outside

Who is the vampire's favorite singer?
Bloody Holly

What did the zombie say to her
boyfriend when he asked to hold
her hand?
OK, but I'm going to need it
back this afternoon.

What do you call a monster who has
stopped moving?
An ambulance

What do they sing to the melting man
on his birthday?
Happy Birthday to EEEWWW!

Why did the Hunchback throw the clock repair man out the window?

He wanted to see Tim fly.

What does the skeleton always order at Red Lobster?

Mussels

Where does the skeleton get it's laundry done?

Bone Dry Cleaning

Why are there only two employees working there?

It's a skeleton crew.

What do you call a bunch of bones wearing a neck-tie?

The skeleton's boss

Now quit cracking jokes and get back to work!

Buddy Onionring

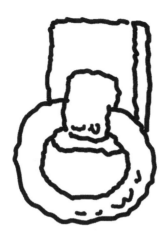

KNOCK-KNOCK
Jokes

KNOCK KNOCK
Who's There?
Ice cream
Ice cream who?
Ice cream because
I think this house is haunted!

KNOCK KNOCK
Who's There?
Irish
Irish who?
Irish I was anywhere
but this haunted house!

KNOCK KNOCK

Who's There?

Lettuce

Lettuce who?

Lettuce out of this haunted house!

KNOCK KNOCK

Who's There?

Amanda

Amanda who?

Amanda let us out of this haunted house is here!

KNOCK KNOCK

Who's There?

Thistle

Thistle who?

Thistle be the last time I go near
that haunted house!

Made in the
USA
Columbia, SC